THIS WALKER BOOK BELONGS TO:

Céon Brougton.

For Cynthia Fitzjohn and her class
S.H.

For David and Elizabeth
T.G.

First published 1988 by Walker Books Ltd
87 Vauxhall Walk, London SE11 5HJ

This edition published 1989

This selection © 1988 Sarah Hayes
Illustrations © 1988 Toni Goffe

Printed in Italy by Lito di Roberto Terrazzi

British Library Cataloguing in Publication Data
Clap your hands: finger rhymes.
1. Children's finger play rhymes in English – Anthologies
I. Hayes, Sarah   II. Goffe, Toni
398'.8
ISBN 0-7445-1231-X

CLAP YOUR HANDS
FINGER RHYMES

Chosen by **Sarah Hayes**   *Illustrated by* **Toni Goffe**

CONTENTS

WALKER BOOKS
LONDON

KNOCK AT THE DOOR

Knock at the door.   Peep in.   Lift the latch.   And walk in.

Chin chopper, chin chopper, chin chopper, chin.

HERE IS THE CHURCH

Here is the church,   And here's the steeple.   Open the doors

I AM A COBBLER

I am a cobbler
And this is what I do:
Rap-tap-a-tap
To mend my shoe.

And here he is
Saying his
prayers.

And see all the
people.

Here is the parson
Going upstairs,

TWO FAT GENTLEMEN

Two fat gentlemen met in a lane,

Bowed most politely,

bowed once again.

How do you do,
How do you do,
And how do you do again?

Two thin ladies met in a lane,
Bowed most politely, bowed once again.
How do you do,
How do you do,
And how do you do again?

Two tall policemen met in a lane,
Bowed most politely, bowed once again.
How do you do,
How do you do,
And how do you do again?

Two little schoolboys met in a lane,
Bowed most politely, bowed once again.
How do you do,
How do you do,
And how do you do again?

Two little babies met in a lane,
Bowed most politely, bowed once again.
How do you do,
How do you do,
And how do you do again?

TEN GALLOPING HORSES

Ten galloping horses came through the town.

Five were white and five were brown.

They galloped up

and galloped down;

Ten galloping horses came through the town.

THE BEEHIVE

Here is the beehive,
Where are the bees?
Hidden away where
nobody sees.

Soon they come creeping
Out of the hive.

One and two and three,
four, five.

LITTLE MOUSIE

Here's a little mousie
Peeking through a hole.

Peek to the left.

Peek to the right.

Pull your
head back in,

There's a
cat
in
sight!

MOUSE IN A HOLE

A mouse lived in
a little hole,

Lived softly in
a little hole,

When all was quiet
as quiet
can be...

OUT
POPPED
HE!

THREE LITTLE MONKEYS

Three little monkeys
Swinging from a tree,

Teasing Mr Alligator,
"Can't catch me!"

Along came Mr Alligator

Slowly as can be...

Then...

SNAP!

INCEY WINCEY SPIDER

Incey wincey spider
climbed up the water spout.

Down came the rain
and washed the spider out.

Out came the sun,
and dried up all the rain.

And incey wincey spider
climbed up the spout again.

CHOOK, CHOOK; CHOOK-CHOOK-CHOOK

Chook, chook; chook-chook-chook,

Good morning, Mrs Hen.

How many chickens have you got?

Madam, I've got ten.

Four of them are yellow,

And four of them
are brown,

And two of them
are speckled red—

The nicest in the town!

GOOD THINGS TO EAT

Will you have
a cookie,

Or a piece
of pie,

Or a striped
candy stick?

Well, so
will I.

THREE LITTLE PUMPKINS

Three little
pumpkins sitting
on a wall,

A witch
came
riding by —

Ha-ha-ha!
I'll take you all
To make a
pumpkin pie!

FIVE FAT PEAS

Five fat peas in a pea-pod pressed.

One grew,   two grew,   so did all the rest.

They grew   and did not   Until one day
and grew   stop,   the pod went POP!

TEN FAT SAUSAGES

Ten fat sausages
sizzling in the pan,
Ten fat sausages
sizzling in the pan,

One went POP

and another went BANG.

There were eight fat sausages sizzling in the pan.

Eight fat sausages sizzling in the pan...

Six fat sausages sizzling in the pan...

Four fat sausages sizzling in the pan...

Two fat sausages sizzling in the pan,
Two fat sausages sizzling in the pan,
One went POP and another went BANG.
There were no fat sausages sizzling in the pan.

THE PANCAKE

Mix a pancake,
Stir a pancake,

Pop it in
the pan.

Fry the
pancake,

Toss the
pancake,

Catch it if you can.

PAT-A-CAKE

Pat-a-cake, pat-a-cake, baker's man,

Bake me a cake as fast as you can.

Pat it

and prick it,

22

and mark it with B,

And put it in the oven for Baby and me.

LITTLE TURTLE

There was a little turtle.

He lived in a box.

He swam in a puddle.

He climbed on the rocks.

He snapped at a mosquito.
He snapped at a flea.
He snapped at a minnow.
He snapped at me.

He caught the mosquito.
He caught the flea.
He caught the minnow.
But he didn't catch me.

ONE, TWO, THREE, FOUR, FIVE

One, two, three, four, five,

Once I caught a fish alive.

Six, seven, eight, nine, ten,

Then I let him go again.

Why did you let him go?
Because he bit my finger so.

Which finger did he bite?
This little finger on the right.

LITTLE ARABELLA MILLER

Little Arabella Miller
Found a woolly caterpillar.
First it crawled upon her mother,

Then upon her
baby brother.

All said,
"Arabella Miller,
Take away that
caterpillar!"

ROUND AND ROUND THE GARDEN

Round and round the garden, like a teddy bear;

One step,   two step,

Tickly under there!

IN A COTTAGE

In a cottage
in a wood

A little old man
at the window stood

Saw a rabbit
running by

Knocking
at the
window.

"Help me!
Help me! Help!"
he said,

"Lest the
huntsman shoot
me dead."

"Come little rabbit,
Come to me,
Happy you shall be."

HOW MANY

How many people live at your house?

One, my mother,

Two, my father,   Three, my sister,

Four, my brother.   There's one more,
                          now let me see.

Oh yes, of course. It must be me!

MORE WALKER PAPERBACKS

THE PRE-SCHOOL YEARS

**John Satchwell
& Katy Sleight**
Monster Maths
ODD ONE OUT   BIG AND LITTLE
COUNTING   SHAPES

FOR THE VERY YOUNG

Byron Barton
TRAINS   TRUCKS   BOATS
AEROPLANES

PICTURE BOOKS
For All Ages

Colin West
"HELLO, GREAT BIG BULLFROG!"
"PARDON?" SAID THE GIRAFFE
"HAVE YOU SEEN THE CROCODILE?"
"NOT ME," SAID THE MONKEY

Bob Graham
THE RED WOOLLEN BLANKET

**Russell Hoban
& Colin McNaughton**
The Hungry Three
THEY CAME FROM AARGH!
THE GREAT FRUIT GUM ROBBERY

Jill Murphy
FIVE MINUTES' PEACE

**Philippa Pearce
& John Lawrence**
EMILY'S OWN ELEPHANT

**David Lloyd
& Charlotte Voake**
THE RIDICULOUS STORY OF
GAMMER GURTON'S NEEDLE

Nicola Bayley
Copycats
SPIDER CAT   PARROT CAT
POLAR BEAR CAT   ELEPHANT CAT
CRAB CAT

**Michael Rosen
& Quentin Blake**
Scrapbooks
SMELLY JELLY SMELLY JELLY
(THE SEASIDE BOOK)

HARD-BOILED LEGS
(THE BREAKFAST BOOK)

SPOLLYOLLYDIDDLYTIDDLYITIS
(THE DOCTOR BOOK)

UNDER THE BED
(THE BEDTIME BOOK)

Jan Ormerod
THE STORY OF CHICKEN LICKEN

**Bamber Gascoigne
& Joseph Wright**
BOOK OF AMAZING FACTS 1

Martin Handford
WHERE'S WALLY?